T0068245

Meet the Road

On the Road Series

LOUISE A. LYONS

WESTBOW
PRESS®
A DIVISION OF THOMAS NELSON
& ZONDERVAN

WestBow Press books may be ordered through booksellers or by contacting:

WestBow Press
A Division of Thomas Nelson & Zondervan
1663 Liberty Drive
Bloomington, IN 47403
www.westbowpress.com
844-714-3454

ISBN: 978-1-6642-4206-7 (sc)
ISBN: 978-1-6642-4207-4 (e)

Library of Congress Control Number: 2021915830

Print information available on the last page.

WestBow Press rev. date: 3/16/2022

Dedication

I dedicate this book to my dear friend, Janice Hill,
my fellow dreamer and inspiration for this series.

Contents

Chapter 1

"I can't believe we are actually doing this," Ann said, sitting in the passenger's seat of a brand-new leisure travel van. She and Faye were waiting for the money to be transferred from their bank to the New Braunfels dealership. Ann had just turned sixty-three, and her complexion was still clear and smooth, with barely any wrinkles. Her curly red hair reached her shoulders, and her spunk was evident in her lively eyes. She sat back in the leather seat and took in the view of the cabin. It was a miniature home.

She and Faye had dreamed of having a van and had only hoped to have a shower in it, but this van had an entire bathroom! The kitchen was beyond their dreams, with a roomy galley that included a refrigerator with a freezer—not some dinky fridge but one the size she had when she was a child. It was smaller than most home refrigerators these days but much larger than most van refrigerators.

The bedroom was beyond the kitchen and bathroom in the rear of the van, with twin beds on either side. Between the beds was a bedside table and a perfect area under the table for Jaz's bed, Ann's miniature dachshund. There were closets for both Ann and Faye to hang their clothes.

"I'm so excited, I don't think I can drive," Ann said, looking at Faye, who was already sitting in the driver's captain chair. Faye reeked of confidence with her back straight and shoulders back, not a hair out of place. She was very attractive, Ann thought, with her blond hair frosted and cut short.

"You are already in the driver's seat, Faye, and you do look outstanding," Ann said.

Faye gave Ann the eye and then smiled. "You know you amaze me," Faye said. "I have seen you overcome so much, but here you are, scared to drive this van."

"I'm not scared—just excited! All this energy has made me shaky," Ann said, holding out her hands, which were shaking. "I don't have the concentration to drive safely." Faye nodded her head in agreement, and Ann added with a bit of a whine, "Besides, you are the driver most of the time in our SUV."

"I got this," Faye said.

"I knew you would. You know, out of the two of us, you are braver. You do things I could never do."

"Ladies," interrupted the young salesman. Both women had decided James was most likely a wonderful son to some lucky mother. He had treated them with the utmost respect. Some may have been suspicious that his treatment was due to their cash purchase of the Unity Twin Bed model, but both ladies had accurate discernment of people. He had confirmed their insight through conversation over the past weeks. James spoke highly of his mother, who was an integral part of his life, and his respectful behavior was relaxed and not forced.

James handed Faye a set of keys. "To your leisure travel van, ladies."

Both women giggled and smiled broadly. "Oh, James, you have been so helpful," Ann said. "I'm not sure we will remember everything you have attempted to teach us about—oh, my," Ann said, looking at Faye. Tears streamed down her cheeks. "About our new traveling home," she finally finished.

"Don't you worry, Ms. Ann," James replied. "You have my card, and feel free to call me anytime you have a question."

Faye patted Ann's knee and said, "And we have the manual. We'll be fine."

"I'm going to miss seeing you, ladies. You both have been the highlight of my day. I hope you will keep me posted on your travels."

"I'll send you a copy of my first book based on our travels," Ann said, wiping her cheeks with a tissue. "Do I have mascara running?" she whispered to Faye, who shook her head no.

Chapter 2

After goodbyes and waves, the ladies pulled out of the dealer's lot onto the main road. "That wasn't so hard," Faye said as they cruised down the feeder road beside the freeway.

Ann giggled and said, "I guess not, since there wasn't another car in sight." She could see Faye give her a look, though she kept her eyes on the road. Ann settled back in her seat and kept quiet, allowing Faye to concentrate.

"Would you please stick your head out the window to see if there are any cars beside me?" Faye asked. "I need to change lanes. I'm not sure if my mirror gets everything beside me."

"Sure," Ann said, rolling her window down. The warm, dry air met her face as she stuck it out the passenger window. The pungent smell of ragweed tickled her nose. She turned her head to look behind her, causing her eyes to water from the fast-blowing breeze. Popping her head back in the cab, she started to laugh.

"What's so funny?" Faye asked. She was not able to stifle a smile as she looked at Ann with windblown hair and joined in the laughter.

Tears rolled down Ann's cheeks, and she began to cough from laughing so hard. She held her hand up and tried to catch her breath. "I stuck my tongue out like a dog to see why dogs loved putting their heads out the window. Then I noticed a car at the stop sign about to turn on the road. I can't imagine what they were thinking when they saw me!"

Ann demonstrated. Faye went into a fit of laughter. "Ann, I'm driving! You are so going to get it! Now we missed our turn."

"Oops," replied Ann.

Once back on track, heading down a farm road to their property, Faye said, "That was pretty funny. You kill me, Ann."

As they drove in comfortable silence, Ann stared out the window, thinking about how this adventure with Faye had begun. Over the years, they had often spoke about traveling the country in a van. When they found themselves widowed, they began considering their dream more seriously. Faye visited Ann regularly in New Braunfels after her husband Gerry's fatal automobile accident.

Faye loved the fellowship that met at Ann's home. She had never experienced the body of Christ in such a loving community. They were all there for one another, sharing all they had as needed. No one in the fellowship lacked anything. The love she received was just what she needed as she grieved the loss of her husband. Ann invited her to move in with her, but Faye was still nursing in Houston.

The Lord nudged Faye when her son had a financial crisis of sorts. Faye, being a generous, compassionate woman, suggested that he move into her home to lower his expenses. She felt his family would better use her four-bedroom home than her living all by herself. She figured she could move into an apartment.

However, Ann suggested that Faye pray about moving in with her. Faye *did* sense God leading her to move in with Ann. She found she was very welcome and felt at home. One thing led to another, and the ladies agreed to pool some of their money to buy a travel van and live their dream.

Ann's husband, Edward, her senior of fifteen years, had died of a heart attack five years earlier, leaving her a substantial retirement and life insurance policy. She also collected royalties from a series of published children's stories.

Ann smiled as Faye expertly turned the van into their shell driveway. "You were made to drive this van," Ann said.

"Thank you. I do enjoy driving it," Faye replied. She pulled into a carport built just for the van.

Later that evening, the ladies were sitting on the back porch of their quaint cottage. "There's nothing more beautiful than a sunset or sunrise," Faye said, sipping on a hazelnut latte.

"I must agree. Just look at that sky," Ann replied. She was sitting in a cushioned white wicker chair with Jaz curled up on her lap. Beyond the cliff overlooking a river below, the sun was setting behind some hills. The sun's partial globe glowed bright orange, while the sky above it was a kaleidoscope of pinks, oranges, and reds. Ann looked at Faye and said, "I am so glad you moved here. You are such a dear. I hope you are as happy as me."

"Of course, I am," Faye replied.

"Edward always enjoyed a beautiful sunset," Ann said with a bit of a catch in her voice.

Faye reached over and laid her hand on Ann's. "I'm sure you miss him."

Ann turned and looked at Faye with a tear running down her cheek, "Yes, I do. Even after five years. Though in a sense, I feel he is still here because he left such a legacy. Every time the fellowship meets, I see him in everything. I am very thankful that God enabled him to provide so well so that I can keep going forward with the vision God gave him."

"I'm certainly blessed to be part of this community that demonstrates the body of Christ. I'll tell you what—I'm excited about the upcoming adventures. Though it is always an adventure living with you." They giggled and silently watched the sun disappear.

A slight chill hung in the September air, so they retreated inside to a cozy living room. Jaz's sleek red body shot through the French doors, and she jumped into her bed that lay beside Ann's chair. "You should have named her Bullet," Faye said.

Chapter 3

The next morning Ann entered the kitchen, rubbing her eyes. Aiming for the coffee machine, she noticed the kitchen and living room were empty. She glanced out the window over the sink while she opened the cabinet to grab a coffee pod. No, Faye wasn't sipping her coffee on the porch. "Hmm, where could she be?" Ann asked Jaz, who was standing at her heels waiting for her breakfast. Faye always left a note or told her if she was going somewhere. Ann glanced on the counter island where Faye typically left her messages. None.

Ann left her coffee to brew and walked down the hall toward Faye's bedroom. *Swoosh, swoosh. I do wish my slippers didn't make so much noise,* she thought. Ann didn't have to knock on Faye's door because it was open. "Faye?" Ann called, standing in the door frame. Nothing. Faye had made her bed, which meant she had started her day.

Jaz made a tiny squeak, and Ann looked down at her wagging her little tail. Her squeak turned into one small bark. "All right, Jaz," she said. Ann turned and began walking back to the kitchen. "Jaz, is that all you think about—your stomach? Don't you wonder where Faye is?" She opened the pantry and retrieved a can of Jaz's favorite dog food. "Something could be wrong," she said, looking down at her dog. Opening the container, she scooped the contents into the ceramic food bowl and squatted next to the doggie mat. "Don't you care?" she asked, scratching the top of Jaz's head. Jaz's long little red-brown body shook as her tail sped up, and she eyed the bowl. Ann finally set the bowl down, and Jaz finished before Ann poured her coffee. "No wonder you are always hungry," Ann said, stirring her coffee. "You never even taste your food."

When Ann opened the door to the patio, Marge was standing at the door with her arm raised and a fist made, about to knock. In her other hand was a square plastic container. "Oops," she said, quickly lowering her arm.

"Good morning, Marge," Ann said. "How are you?"

Marge and her husband, Jim, took care of the grounds and made repairs on the house. Ann and Edward had hired them several years before Edward died. They had become family. They even celebrated holidays together most years.

"I'm good. And you?" Marge answered.

"A bit out of sorts," Ann replied, stepping aside for Marge to enter.

"Oh, my. Why?" Marge placed the plastic container on the island and turned toward Ann with a concerned look on her chubby face.

"Faye is missing."

"Missing? But I just saw her," Marge said as she walked past Ann. Ann stood next to the door stroking Jaz, who cuddled in her arms.

Ann exclaimed, "You did?"

"Yes, she is in the travel van. The side door of the van was open when I walked here. Faye was sitting at the table. That travel van looks wonderful."

"It is," Ann replied. "I will be glad to give you a tour now that you solved the mystery." She made a beeline for the van.

"Ann," Marge called after her, "Jim was in the mood for pecan cinnamon rolls this morning, so I brought you and Faye some."

Ann turned around and walked backward. "Wonderful! Bless Jim!" she exclaimed, throwing her arms up as though someone made a touchdown. "If you like, get Jim, and I'll show both of you the van. Then we can all have coffee and cinnamon rolls."

"Hey, girl," Ann greeted Faye, popping her head around the corner of the open door.

"Good morning. I'm making a list of things to buy at the store for the van."

"Great. What do you say we go after coffee and pecan cinnamon rolls?"

Faye popped her head up and looked at Ann. "Marge baked?"

Ann nodded. She giggled and said, "I can see by your eyes that your salivary glands are activated."

"You bet they are, anytime Marge bakes!"

"I promised them a tour first and invited them to have coffee with us."

Chapter 4

As Jim took a seat at the patio table, he whistled and ran his hand through his reddish-blonde hair. "That is some travel van, ladies. You will be traveling in luxury." He rolled up his shirt sleeves and accepted a mug of steaming hot brew.

"Isn't it?" Ann replied excitedly, entering the patio with a mug also. "I still can't believe we got it."

Faye set a plate filled with cinnamon rolls in the center of the glass table. "Since it hasn't been twenty-four hours that we have had it, I agree," she teased.

Marge stirred some sugar in her coffee and looked at Jim. Ann took a seat across from Marge and Jim and smiled. There he sat, a thin man with reddish-blonde hair and a face full of freckles, but the look in Marge's eyes revealed that she saw the most handsome, wonderful man in the world. She always had a kind word about him, and he did her also.

Marge was a complete contrast from Jim. She was short, plump, and olive-skinned and had dark brown hair. Marge admitted that she also loved her baking—not to mention that, with her Italian heritage, she could cook too.

"Ann," Faye said, staring at her from the chair next to her, "Big Bend, maybe?"

Ann gave Faye a confused look. "Big Bend?"

"Were you in your own world?" Faye asked.

"I guess," Ann replied. "What's this about Big Bend?"

"Jim asked where we might go first. I said maybe Big Bend."

The conversation wrapped up, and Jim and Marge left to work in the vegetable garden. The ladies excitedly chatted for the next thirty minutes about what they may encounter at Big Bend. Ann and Faye finished the list of items for the van that Faye had begun, then off to the store they went. On their return, they carried bags and bags to the van.

"This is so much fun," Ann said, spreading the comforters on the twin beds to the sounds of smooth jazz.

"Tonight, why don't we start planning the first trip?" Faye suggested.

"Great idea. I picked up an atlas in the bookstore the other day."

"Big Bend isn't that far," Faye commented looking at the atlas that evening.

Ann took a seat next to Faye at the table in the breakfast nook. "So how far are we talking?"

"Just a little over six hundred miles," Faye replied, moving her finger along the route on the atlas. "However, there is an additional hour to drive through the park to the place we will be camping."

"So when do we leave?" Ann asked. Jaz sat at Ann's feet, and her tail started to wag. "Not yet. Hold your doggy horses."

"Well, I'll need to make reservations, so that will determine when we go. The place is Rio Grande Village."

Ann pulled up the website on her phone, and Faye leaned in to look at the screen. "There's where to make reservations," Faye said, pointing to a link. Ann pressed it, and the screen flashed and took them to a form.

Ann squealed and bounced up and down in her chair. "We are doing this! We have reserved a spot for October 15th."

Faye laughed and said, "Yes, we will be pulling into Big Bend before you know it. In the meantime, we have plenty to do to get ready."

Time flew by, and they left for their adventure. They arrived at the Rio Grande Village Campsite. Their first go at traveling in their new leisure van would consist of a sort of dry camping—not entirely in the real sense of dry camping, though it would require some flexible camping. *Dry camping* was part of their new lingo. It refers to camping without using water or electrical hookups at the camping site. They were fortunate to reserve a spot where they could use their generator since there were no hookups in the park. But using the generator meant they would need to limit their electrical use since they would be there for fourteen days. They would use the park facilities as well as their own shower and toilet from time to time. Since October temperatures were cool during the night, they would enjoy open windows rather than use air conditioning. Most importantly, their refrigerator, computer, and phone chargers would need electricity.

Their first adventure started the morning after arrival. The sun had risen and was sneaking above the horizon in full view when they set out. The day promised to be beautiful, and both ladies were surprised by the comfortable temperature. But by the time they arrived at the trail's entrance in the Chisos Basin, Faye was wiping sweat from her forehead with her sleeve. She plopped her Cubs cap back on top of her head and leaned on her walking stick, waiting for Ann. The last Faye had seen of Ann was when she had gotten caught up in conversation with another hiker, so Faye had gone ahead. Ann finally caught up, struggling to tie her windbreaker around her waist. Faye smiled at her friend with admiration. Ann had the freedom to be comfortable no matter how silly she looked. For instance, at present, Ann had reduced her headful of curly red hair into a two-inch ponytail that was sticking up on the top of her head.

Chapter 5

They both stood before the sign at the Chisos Basin Trailhead. They read the different trails available, and Ann said, "Faye, I've heard the Pinnacles Trail has a beautiful view of the Window." The Window is a well-known site of some mountain views in the park.

"Yes, me too," Faye replied. "There are so many choices. We will have to keep returning until we have seen them all."

Puffy clouds dotted the blue sky. A light breeze followed the ladies along a rocky dirt path cutting between oak trees.

"Faye," Ann whispered, "look." She pointed to a deer just ten feet away, nibbling on greenery that broke through the ground in spurts.

They both stopped and quietly observed the deer until it had its fill and went on its way. "Oh my, I just love seeing God's creatures upfront in their natural habitat!" Ann squealed.

"Me too," Faye replied and smiled. "I think that was a white-tailed deer."

The birds surrounded them with song. Faye and Ann searched for birds to identify. Ann stopped on the trail, and Faye gave her the binoculars to scan through the trees. Faye started to walk away when Ann called, "Faye, wait! Come look." Ann handed her the binoculars and pointed her toward where she was looking. "Can you see it?"

"What am I looking for?"

"A bird. It is blue and white with a black beak that sticks straight out. Oh, and it has a crest on its head that looks like a Mohawk haircut."

Faye scanned the trees, adjusting the binoculars. "I found it," she said. "That is a belted kingfisher. I was hoping we would see this bird. I've never seen one in the wild."

Faye had been a bird-watcher for years and found great pleasure in studying all her bird books. Before this adventure, she had spent hours researching what birds were in Big Bend.

As they continued, Faye suddenly stopped. Ann stopped beside her. "Listen, Ann."

"I hear it," Ann said quietly. "It's a woodpecker."

Faye scanned the trees and spotted some black and white feathers and a black tail. She zoomed in and saw the bright red and yellow head. "Here," she said, handing Ann the binoculars. "It's a golden-fronted woodpecker."

Not only were the birds astounding, but the views were breathtaking. Both oohed and awed over Ward Mountain, standing proudly in front of them on Pinnacles Trail. The sun beamed down, making the terrain a light rusty brown with streams of green running down like rivers on the sides of the mountain.

Reaching the top of a steep incline of rock stairs, they came to a flattened area. "Oh, look, Faye," Ann said, coming to a halt and taking in some deep breaths. She pointed to a big rock. "Let's sit down and take in this view for a while."

In one direction lay a meadow stretching out to a tall, looming cliff, and in the other were what looked like waves of rocky mountains coming toward them. The fall colors of yellow, orange, and red covered the landscape.

After taking a breather, they decided to venture onto another trail that took them into a forestry area. A carpet of deep green moss lay in front of tall trees. The temperature dropped, leading Ann to slip on her windbreaker. They chose a nearby log to sit on and share a snack while the birds serenaded them.

The rustle of fallen leaves caught Ann's attention. "Do you hear that?" she asked.

The rustle of leaves turned into a shuffling of leaves with an added snorting sound. Both ladies froze. The snorting seemed to be coming from across the path in a heavily wooded and bushy area.

Ann gasped as the source of the snorting came into view. A black bear about four feet tall on all fours was browsing through the vegetation with his brown snout. The ladies looked at each other. "Ann, slowly seal your snack and put it in the backpack," Faye said.

Ann responded with a whine. The bear looked up just as she finished doing as Faye instructed. He snorted loudly and stomped his paws on the ground, sending dirt and leaves flying behind him.

"OK," Faye whispered, "that means the bear wants space. Let's slowly get up and move down the trail."

"Move down the trail?" Ann responded in a hoarse whisper. "You have got to be kidding."

The bear again stomped and swung his head back and forth.

"Wait a minute," Ann whispered. "I don't need to be afraid of this bear. Jesus has authority over everything in heaven and earth, including this bear. And he has given me that authority."

Ann rose from her seat and said aloud, "Bear, go on your way. We mean you no harm." Faye stared at Ann, who was now picking up her backpack. "Come on, Faye, let's get going too."

Faye watched Ann return to the trail and then looked at the bear. He lumbered off in the opposite direction back into the forest of trees.

Chapter 6

"Oh, my," Faye said, quickly grabbing her pack. "Did that just happen?" she asked Ann as she caught up and walked beside her.

"It is amazing to walk in the Spirit, isn't it?" Ann said. "I realized I didn't have to be afraid and that there was no reason to be afraid. Respectful, yes, but not afraid."

"You will have to include this in one of your books," Faye said.

"Yes," Ann agreed. "And what a blessing to have had the privilege to see a real bear in the wild."

They continued walking for some time until they arrived at the end of the trail, where the trail signs promised a scenic view of the Window.

Ann gasped as she took in the view of a cloudless blue sky hanging above an expanse of mountains and desert that seemingly went on forever through this window. The Window was two mountain ranges that intersected and formed a V. They both stood in silence and awe.

When the ladies returned to the van and opened the door, a tiny bundle of joy greeted them. Jaz was wagging her tail enthusiastically, causing her body to tremble. "Hi, baby. Were you a good girl?" Ann said, lifting Jaz and holding her tightly against her chest. Jaz licked Ann's chin as Ann rubbed her cheek against Jaz's jowl. Jaz's tongue went into fast motion, licking every inch of skin on Ann's face, causing her to giggle and squeal.

"We'll be outside. I need to take Jaz out to potty," Ann called to Faye, who had gone to the bathroom.

"OK. I'm going to take a shower."

"OK."

Once outside, Ann set Jaz on the ground, and they walked to a grassy area. She scanned the RV park. Leisure vans, travel vans, and recreational vehicles with trucks filled the park. It was the middle of the afternoon, and a few people were outside doing this and that. She figured most were out enjoying the park just as she and Faye had been. Jaz was busy sniffing what seemed to be of great interest.

"Hello," a man called from across the road as he waved.

Ann waved back and said hello. Jaz suddenly looked up and began running toward the man. "Jaz, stop!" Ann ran after her and scooped her up at the edge of the road. The man stood on the other side.

"What an adorable dog," he said. "Is it a puppy?"

"The way she obeys, you would think so," Ann responded. "But no. Jaz is a toy dachshund." Ann walked across the road with the squirming bundle of energy in her arms.

"My name is Ralph," the man said.

"This is Jaz, and I am Ann."

"Can I pet Jaz?" he asked. Ann nodded. As he stroked Jaz's head, her tail beat Ann's side.

"I didn't know dachshunds could be so small. It's like having a puppy all their life."

"Oh my!" squealed a short, friendly-looking woman approaching them. "Is that a dachshund pup?"

A conversation about toy dachshunds turned to a discussion about hiking, which this couple enjoyed also. Ann discovered that Ralph and Jenny were from the Houston area. "Say, why don't you and your friend join us for dinner," Ralph said. "I was going to grill hamburgers and hot dogs. Throwing a couple more on the grill won't be a bit of trouble. Then we can trade stories."

"That sounds wonderful," Ann replied. "I'll ask Faye if she would like to do that and let you know. Then I'm going to go shower and catch a short nap. I'm pooped."

"I guess so," replied Jenny, "after that many miles of hiking. How about six o'clock? We can build a fire and tell scary stories when it gets dark." She and Ann giggled.

"You think we jest," Ralph said, "but this area has its legends, and even people in the present have experienced some interesting happenings."

"This is sounding better every minute," Ann replied. "I'll go run over and ask Faye and be right back."

The evening was on, and the ladies agreed to bring some chips and sodas.

Chapter 7

"Those were delicious," Faye said as she finished her hamburger. "Was that blue cheese in the center?"

Ralph nodded yes while he scraped the grill, and Jenny replied, "Ralph loves to cook, and he has lots of ways to prepare a hamburger that is far from boring."

Ralph smiled at his wife and asked, "Would anyone care for a glass of wine?"

They all relaxed in lawn chairs around a circle of large stones. They sipped their wine, gazing at the sky of pink streaks crossing a purplish evening sky. The sound of children playing and adults laughing surrounded them. Faye pulled her shawl more tightly around her shoulders. Ralph rose and, looking over at Faye, said, "I believe that is my cue to prepare a fire."

Ralph filled the pit with pine wood, and within minutes, a roaring fire offered its warmth. A crisp, sweet aroma floated in the air.

The setting sun lowered on the horizon and found its resting place, turning the sky ebony black with stars that looked like millions of tiny fireflies.

The flame had settled down and burned much lower, allowing

the darkness more room. "Oh, my, it is extremely dark, even though we have a fire," Ann commented.

Ralph sat in his chair poking at the fire and said, "It gets extremely dark in the park because there aren't any city lights nearby. There aren't any cities nearby, for that matter. I hope you ladies have a flashlight for your return."

"I didn't even think of it," Faye replied.

"We'll walk you back," Jenny assured them.

"Oh my, how beautiful," Ann said, looking up to the sky filled with tiny pinpricks of light and a waning moon.

"There's the Little Dipper," Ralph said, pointing to the right. "And way over there, I believe, is Saturn."

"I've never seen such a clear view of the Little Dipper," Faye replied.

"You ought to go to the McDonald Observatory," Jenny said.

"Oh, yes," Ralph added, "we've gone, and it is terrific. You can stay in a nearby motel overnight. Check with the information center for what they call star parties. They will provide transportation."

"There is so much more to do at Big Bend than I ever imagined," Faye said. "Ann, let's go to the information center tomorrow to see when the next star party takes place."

"When my youngest son was elementary age, he loved astronomy," Ann said. "We made one of those star maps where you poke holes in a piece of paper and hold it up in the night sky. We had so much fun. We bought a telescope for him, which he thoroughly enjoyed."

Soon, they were all talking about their families. Faye and Ann learned that Ralph and Jenny were soon to be grandparents.

Their daughter, Maggie, also lived in the Houston area near where Ralph and Jenny lived. She was almost due to give birth to their first grandchild. The new parents decided to let the sex of the baby be a surprise.

After a while, Ralph asked, "Ladies, are you attending the chili cook-off?

"Chili cook-off?" Ann asked.

Chapter 8

Ralph said, "Do you mean to tell me that you don't know about the chili cook-off? It is the first Saturday in November every year. This year it is November second."

"We're only booked here until November first," Faye said.

Jenny quickly replied, "We stay at BJ's RV Park near Terlingua. Call them tomorrow and see if they have any available spots."

"Honestly," Ralph said, looking at his wife and then the ladies, "everywhere like that is probably booked. It's a big event and draws thousands. If you can't reserve a spot, you can try going to the park where the cook-off takes place. It's first come, first serve there for parking."

"We'd love for you to come and spend a couple of days," Jenny said. "There is lots to do. And get ready to do some dancing."

"I'll call around tomorrow and see if we can find a place to park," Faye said. "That is, if you would like to go, Ann?

"Yes, I think that would be fun," she answered.

Ralph rubbed his hands together and said, "Now that we have settled that, let's get on to the high point of the night."

Faye and Ann stared at Ralph while Jenny donned a big smile.

Then Ralph put his finger to his lips and said, "Shh, I think I hear something."

They all quietly listened. There weren't any sounds. The children had gone in, and no one else was making any noise.

"I don't hear anything," whispered Ann.

"There!" Ralph exclaimed in a loud whisper. "It sounded like a branch snapping!"

"You don't think it's a bear, do you?" Jenny said seriously.

"I'm afraid not," Ralph answered. "I suspect something otherworldly."

"Otherworldly?" Faye asked.

"I guess you haven't heard the rumors about this area?"

Ralph proceeded to tell the local folklore as the darkness cloaked them around the campfire. The crackling occasionally ran a chill down Faye's back.

"Witches Canyon has had the most reports from fellow campers. You see," Ralph said, pausing for several seconds before continuing, "there was a beautiful Apache maiden whom Mexican bandits had pursued. Foolishly, she had separated herself from those she was traveling with by wandering off while daydreaming. The bandits spotted her from a distance. She saw them and knew they wanted to capture her and would make sport of her, so she ran with all her might to where the river flowed like a torrent. She watched the water rush past her over rocks. The river was high at that time of year. No one attempted to cross at that spot because they knew they would not make it to the other side. The bandits were in her sights. She jumped into the river, which swallowed her in minutes. By the time the bandits arrived, there was no sight of her, only a loud, eerie moan echoed in the canyon. Today, some who have visited the canyon claim to have heard the maiden's moan."

"How sad," Ann said. "Is that a true story?"

It's the local folklore," Ralph replied, "but as I said, there have been reports of a moaning heard in that area."

"OK, Ralph," Jenny chided, "don't you think that is enough eerie stories? The ladies have to walk back in the dark."

"Oh, my, you're not walking back with us?" Ann asked, alarmed.

"You have Jaz there to protect you," Ralph said with a smile.

Jaz's ears raised along with her head, and she let out a tiny bark. They all laughed, which set Jaz off wagging her tail and readying to jump off Ann's lap. "No, you don't, Jaz. I will set you down," she said, lowering Jaz on the ground.

"Thank you for walking us back to our van," Faye said to Ralph as he pointed the flashlight at the door.

"No problem. We had a wonderful time. I hope I didn't scare you too much with the ghost story."

"Nothing to worry about here. We have Jaz to ward off ghosts and bandits!" Faye said, opening the door.

Chapter 9

"What a beautiful morning," Faye said as she approached Ralph, who was checking his engine. "Ann and I have had so much fun hiking with you and Jenny this week." She was carrying a plastic container, and Ann had a large thermos.

"And what do we have here, ladies?" Ralph asked, wiping his hands on a rag.

Ann said with a giggle, "Just some of the best cinnamon rolls you will ever taste."

"And if you drink this coffee," Faye said, pointing to the thermos, "not one calorie will stick."

"Did I hear *coffee*?" Jenny said, coming out the side door. "You are a godsend. We ran out of coffee this morning after only one cup."

"That will never do," Ann said. "Just count on us to supply your coffee until we all leave."

The ladies laid out the morning goodies, and everyone sat at the picnic table.

"Mmm!" Jenny said. "Oh, my, you were not kidding. These are the best cinnamon rolls I have ever tasted."

"I wish I could take all the credit, but the recipe is Marge's,"

Ann said. "She and her husband are members of our community fellowship. She is an excellent cook and baker and supplies the community with baked goods."

"They also are caretakers who work for us," Faye added. "They help keep up our place and attend to the garden that supplies the veggies for our community."

The only sounds heard from Ralph were *mmm*s and *ahh*s. The ladies looked at one another and broke out laughing.

"What?" Ralph said innocently, his mouth stuffed with a cinnamon roll.

"You'll have to tell me more about this community," Jenny said.

"We," Ann said, looking Faye's way, "have been part of a fellowship for years. My husband was one of the pastors. We believe the church is the people, not a building. We live out what Jesus taught the first disciples. We meet once a week as a group to share a meal and fellowship. The rest of the week, we are involved in one another's life like a family."

"Because we are family," Faye added.

Jenny's phone rang, and she answered. A few minutes into the conversation, she looked worried and said, "We'll be there as soon as we can. Please keep us updated, Charles."

Jenny hung up, and Ralph asked, "What is it?"

"Maggie's at the hospital. Her water broke."

"But she's three weeks early!" Ralph exclaimed.

"They are going to induce labor since her water broke," Jenny explained. "Otherwise, an infection could set in. Now, Ralph, we need to be calm. Everything will be just fine."

"Well, then, we need to get back," Ralph concluded.

"I told Charles we would be there as soon as possible."

"Is there anything we can do to help you get on the road sooner?" Faye asked.

"How about we say a prayer together?" Ann suggested.

They all held hands, and Ann led them in prayer. "Lord, we ask you to protect both child and mother. Give the doctor wisdom."

"Thank you," both Jenny and Ralph said.

"Oh, no!" Ralph exclaimed. "We won't be able to attend the chili cook-off. How about we call BJ's and see if you ladies can have our spot? That way, you can go to the cook-off."

"How very nice," Faye replied.

After some rushed preparations, Ralph and Jenny pulled out, waving goodbye to Faye and Ann. Ann waved Jaz's front paw to say goodbye. They had exchanged phone numbers and promised to be in touch to share updates on both the new baby and what the ladies thought about the cook-off.

Later that week, the ladies drove past a desert floor covered in a sea of cowboy hats blending in with awnings and tents protruding from campers and travel vans. They pulled into BJ's, which was directly next to where the chili cook-off would take place. Faye parked and went to the office while Ann took Jaz out to potty. Jaz stopped in her tracks, sniffing the air. The smell of beef floating from row upon row of cooktops was of more interest to her than going to the bathroom.

"It does smell good, girl," Ann said, taking in the view. The land was barren of vegetation except for a patch of scrub brush here and there. However, if RVs were flowers, there was no lack. RVs of every kind filled the once-vacant acreage along with a group of tents just over a dune.

Chapter 10

"OK, we're all set," Faye announced, approaching the van with a map in hand. "Let's get parked, and then we can get hooked up."

Faye pulled up to their site. "Thank goodness I've got lots of room. I have to back this RV into that space."

Ann looked at Faye wide-eyed. "You mean as in reverse?"

Faye nodded and pulled forward. "Can you get out and direct me?" she asked. "Go to the back and wave your hands. I will toot the horn if I can see you. Then direct me near the connections."

Ann quickly exited the RV and went to the rear. She waved and was relieved to hear the horn. She surveyed their spot and found the obvious connections.

Faye joined Ann next to the connections with a clipboard in hand. "Did you set the parking brake and chock the wheels?" Ann asked.

Faye checked off the task and replied, "Done."

They continued with the procedures on the list. "This is hard," Ann said.

"Yes, but we can do this with the Lord working through us," Faye said. "However, I think I am going to go to the office and get help. I'm a bit nervous hooking up to the right receptacle that matches our amperage."

The gentleman working at the park office was kind enough to go through the entire process of hooking up the RV with Faye and Ann.

"Yes, the water is hot. It heated up pretty fast," Faye said after turning off the hot water spigot. "I will never be able to thank you for all your help, Martin."

Faye shook Martin's hand and slipped a couple of twenties in it.

"That isn't necessary," Martin said.

"There will be no arguments," Faye insisted.

The ladies both agreed that next on the agenda was to relax. They set up their comfy yard chairs under the RV awning and sipped homemade lemonade they had made fresh that morning.

"God is so faithful to provide all we need," Faye said. "Martin was a blessing.

"He sure was," Ann agreed. "I know we had the manual, but, wow, with all the hookups needed, it was great to have help. Using the generator at the last place was so much easier."

"We sure made the right decision to empty our black and gray water before we left Big Bend," Faye added. "Let's make that a practice. One less thing to do when setting up."

"Agreed," Ann said, holding her glass of lemonade up like she was making a toast. Faye lifted her glass and met Ann's with a *ching*.

"What a sight," Faye said, pointing to the area in front of

them. "I bet it is even hotter over there with all that chili cooking in this scorching sun."

Faye was undoubtedly right about it being hotter amid the chili cooking in the crowd. However, a stop in front of a tent with a fan allowed them to meet some interesting people. The chili paraphernalia was everywhere—everything from buttons worn like badges to T-shirts declaring the wearers as "chiliheads." If the attendees had animals, they also advertised their chili beliefs. Among the strangers, laughter rang out along with country music blaring from radios throughout. The air was permeated with the smell of cooked beef, making the ladies' stomachs growl. They were disappointed to discover that they would not be consuming any of the delicious-smelling chili as it was only for the judges. A potluck at Cowboy Camp that evening would make a sufficient consolation. They were glad they had eaten earlier in the day.

"We can pull out the grill when we get back," Faye said, "which ought to be soon because I'm getting hungry."

"Sounds great to me," Ann replied and then stood there staring ahead.

"What do you see?" Faye asked.

Ann pointed to a tent just ahead and said, "I think that is Dan, an old friend."

"I recall Dan. Didn't he have a wife who became ill?"

"Yes. After her death, Edward and I lost touch with him," Ann said. "He threw himself into his work and was traveling most of the time."

"Shall we go say hello?"

"Yes, let's do," Ann replied with a smile.

As she and Faye approached, Dan saw Ann and said, "Oh, my, is that you, Lil' Annie?"

She had acquired this nickname when she and Edward had attended the play *Little Orphan Annie* with Dan and his wife years earlier. Orphan Annie and Ann both had bright red hair.

"Hello, Dan." Ann looked him up and down as he stood behind a card table dressed in baggy denim shorts and a T-shirt with a picture of jalapenos and a bowl of chili. The words "Hot and Spicy" stretched across his chest. His smile revealed that he still had his perfect white teeth. She had always envied him those teeth since hers were crooked.

Dan quickly came around the table and took Ann into his arms for a hug. He held her by her shoulders and stepped back. "Who would have thought we would run into each other here of all places!"

Chapter 11

"It's great to see you, Dan," Ann said. Dan released her, and she stepped aside. "You remember Faye, don't you?"

"Yes, yes, of course," he replied, extending his hand, which Faye shook. "So, girls, where are the boys?"

Faye and Ann looked at each other, and there was an uncomfortable silence until Faye said, "Sadly, they have both passed away."

"Oh, I am sorry," Dan said. "And I am sorry we lost touch," he said to Ann. "Edward was a good man. He was a good friend to me. He always had time for me. After Mary's death, I just was lost. I took a new position with a different company, threw myself into work, and traveled most of the time. I was trying to get rid of everything that reminded me of Mary. I was angry and bitter after watching her die such an agonizing death. Edward attempted to reach out to me, but I made myself unavailable. Before I knew it, we had drifted apart, and I lost contact."

"Most likely because we moved to New Braunfels," Ann said. "The last time Edward tried to call you, the number had been disconnected."

"Yes, I had moved," Dan said. "As I said, I made myself unavailable. I'm truly sorry."

"It's fine," Ann said, patting his arm. "He never stopped praying for you. And he understood your hurt."

"Well, so," Dan said, "is this your first chili cook-off?"

"Yes," Faye responded. "And we were surprised we wouldn't get to try anyone's chili."

"Those along this row," he said, pointing, "take the remaining chili after the judging and add all the other goodies one expects in chili. Then we have our potluck right here. I'd love for you ladies to join us. Then we can go over to Krazy Flats. There's a big time there with music and dancing."

"That sounds wonderful," Faye said, looking at Ann, who was already nodding her head in agreement. "We have some hot dogs and buns we could contribute."

"OK, then," Dan said. "We will meet back here, say at six o'clock tomorrow. The judging should be over by then."

"We will see you then," Ann said.

Faye and Ann returned to their cozy RV. That night they both slept soundly.

It was an exciting day, and the judges had chosen their winners for the CASI cook-off. Dan came in fourth. Though Faye and Ann didn't get to taste any of the chili from that cook-off, they did get to taste some from other cook-offs. These were the people who didn't get into Terlingua's main competition but still wanted to compete. There were also barbecue, beans, and black-eyed pea cook-offs. As the potluck approached, the ladies weren't sure they could eat much more. But they were determined to try Dan's chili, so they prepared their plates with hot dogs smothered in chili and onions.

"Oh, my, if this chili was fourth, I can't imagine what first place tasted like," Ann said with a mouthful of hot dog and chili. "Oh, I'm so sorry," she said, holding a napkin to her mouth.

"Did you ladies come down here just for the chili cook-off?" Dan asked.

"We planned a stay at Big Bend. While we were there, we met a couple and became fast friends," Faye said, smiling. "And they told us about the cook-off."

"They were a lovely couple," Ann said. "They also told us about McDonald's Observatory, which we hope to visit."

"The observatory is great. There is a group here that buys tickets for a star party." Dan hollered toward a man sitting at the tent next to his, "Rick, do you know if there are any tickets left for tonight's star party?"

"You are in luck, buddy. We have four more tickets and also have booked rooms for the ticket holders," Rick replied. "We thought we were going to take a loss this year."

"We'll take three tickets and two rooms," Dan replied.

Rick pulled out his cell phone, and before they had all finished their hot dogs, he had made the arrangements.

Chapter 12

As evening approached, they boarded one of several vans provided for the star party participants. Dan took the ladies' overnight bags and loaded them onto the shelf provided for luggage. Ann had Jaz in the pup's travel bag and held her in her lap. Jaz stuck her head out but knew to stay still while in her bag.

"She is certainly adorable," Dan said, sitting in the seat across the aisle from Faye and Ann.

"Jaz is a good girl," Ann said in doggy speak, scratching the dog's head. "She likes to travel," Ann said, looking down at Jaz with adoration.

"Faye," Dan said, "you are certainly quiet. Is everything all right?"

"Yes. I think I'm just tired and could use a cup of coffee," she replied. "It's been a long busy day. And I'm stuffed," she added, patting her stomach.

"They will have refreshments at the party, and coffee is one of them," Dan said.

"I still can hardly believe how blessed we are to have gotten tickets," Ann said. "We have certainly seen the Lord's favor on us during this trip."

When they arrived at the motel in Marfa two and a half hours later, the sun had set. They quickly dropped their bags off in their rooms. Ann got Jaz comfortable in her pillow bed and set out a bowl of water and crunchies.

"We'll be back soon, sweetie," Ann said, petting Jaz. She clicked the TV remote and found the nature channel.

They again boarded a van for the drive to Dark Sky Drive located in the Davis Mountains. Excitement was in the air and went up a notch as the domes came into view. The van drove up to the visitor's center, and the guide ushered them into the lobby, where Faye found her coffee.

"Ladies and gentlemen," announced the hostess to the group, "we have a no light policy so everyone can see the night sky without any light compromising the view. So please turn off your cell phones and do not use your cameras."

The guide led them into a pitch-black area inside the dome. "I can finally see," Ann whispered, looking up into the night sky. "It is amazing!" The three of them gazed up at the night sky while they waited their turn in line at the telescope.

"You must see this, Faye. It's Saturn. You can see the rings," Ann said with her eye pressed against the eyepiece. She stepped aside for Faye to see.

Back out in the open air, Dan pointed out some constellations, and they excitedly chatted about the wondrous universe God created. "And God has made way for us to see some of it," Faye said.

"Yes. It's crazy to think that humans were able to invent a tool that could see so far away," Ann added.

"Not to mention," Dan interjected, "that he has given us the knowledge and understanding to travel in the universe."

"I certainly had a splendid time," Faye said as they exited the van in front of their motel.

"Me too!" Ann exclaimed. "Dan, what time does the van arrive to return us to Terlingua?"

"Eight o clock, so we will need to meet for breakfast at, say, seven fifteen?"

Ann and Faye looked at each other and nodded in agreement. "Sounds great. I'm going to our room. I'm tired," Ann said to Faye.

"Faye, are you too tired to sit in the lobby and chat a while?" Dan asked.

Faye could tell that Ann had picked up on something she had missed because Ann had already started walking to the hall leading to their room. It was at this moment that Faye realized Dan might be interested in her as more than a friend. Did she want to allow Dan into her life?

"That would be nice," Faye responded, thinking that until she got to know him, she could not very well decide if she wanted him in her life.